Christmas Queens

By

Alicia Lane Dutton

Christmas Queens Cast
7F/2M

Louise Ledbetter: 40-70, Owns Louise's Limelight Theater
Buck Jackson: 40-60, Smart, gentleman catfish farmer, widow
Jolene "Skye" Newcomb: 18-mid 20's, Truly a pageant queen
CeCe Whitlow: 30-40, Very pregnant
Belva Pike: 60-80, Sweet, loves to travel
Tammy Jo Fordham: 40-60, Beautiful, soap opera star
Norma Fay Jones: 50-60, Tough, independent woman
Allison (Allie) Pettigrew: 20's, Just out of college
Cooper Tatum: 20's, Aspires to make documentaries

Synopsis

This year, the Catoosa County Christmas Queen Pageant, sponsored by a local catfish farmer, will invite former winners to compete in a special reunion pageant. Louise, owner of The Limelight Theater, isn't thrilled with the idea but needs the sponsorship money. The former queens range in age from 19 to Belva's not telling. Unfortunately, someone is sabotaging the competition. Is it the oldest queen? The soap opera star? The pregnant competitor, or any of the other women competing for the prize money?

Unit Set

Dressing Room in Louise's Limelight Theater
Tequila Mockingbird Bar and Grill

ACT I
Scene 1

Dressing room of Louise's Limelight Theater.
Louise is cleaning the counter. Buck is
pacing nervously.

BUCK
I don't know Louise. This year I really want it to be
special.
LOUISE
I think it's special every year, Buck.
BUCK
That's not what I mean. It's the fiftieth anniversary
of the pageant and I've been sponsoring the dang thing
the last ten years so I want it to be REALLY special.
LOUISE
Really special, as in Bubba Bronson special?
BUCK
Now Louise.
LOUISE
I mean, I'd say any man who believes he's the
reincarnation of Marilyn Monroe is REALLY special. He
gets on my nerves.
BUCK
Be nice, Louise. That boy hasn't done a thing to you.
LOUISE
He has offended my ladylike sensibilities. As a matter
of fact, he offends them all the time. Nine times out
of ten when I'm driving down Highway thirty-one, he's
standing outside smoking one of those long cigarettes
in some outlandish outfit. I drove by one time and he
had on a white dress letting the dryer vent blow the
skirt up, trying to be a Marilyn Monroe pin up or
something. It was scandalous.

BUCK
I don't know how that could be vulgar enough to offend
your sensibilities. He always wears sweatpants under
his dresses.
LOUISE
Only because May Nell told him that if he didn't, he
couldn't live there anymore.
BUCK
It's good she's got him to take care of her after the
chainsaw accident.
LOUISE
I told May Nell to stop trying to juggle those chain
saws. She's lucky she only lost a foot.
BUCK
I don't know what you've got against Bubba. Obviously
he's a good boy taking care of his Momma. And as far as
thinking he's Marilyn Monroe reincarnated, when he sang
Diamonds are a Girl's Best Friend at half time after
the band got the bird flu, he almost had me convinced.
LOUISE
You better watch it, Buck. You keep on talking like
that and people'll think you're like those weirdo
Californians. We'll have to ship you out there with (in
a sultry voice) Dr. Veronica Devereaux.
BUCK
Her name is Tammy Jo and she's not like that.
LOUISE
You don't think all those years in California will
change a girl?
BUCK
Speaking of Tammy Jo, didn't she win this pageant one
year?
LOUISE
Yes she did, right before she took off out west to find
fame and fortune. She didn't deserve it if you ask me.

She always had a strange looking nose.
BUCK
What?!
LOUISE
Yep, after she won Catoosa County Christmas Queen she
didn't even have the decency to come back and crown the
next year's winner. I don't figure she'll ever leave
California. I mean, what would "Hot Springs General
Hospital" do without their Jezebel doctor?
BUCK
She's not really a Jezebel, Louise. She just plays one
on T.V.
LOUISE
You don't know that. If she ever comes back to Catoosa
County maybe you'll find out.
BUCK
That's it! What, if not just Tammy Jo came back, but we
had a bunch of the former Catoosa County Christmas
Queens come back.
LOUISE
Why in the world would they come back? I think they all
still live here except for.. (sultry) Dr. Devereaux.
BUCK
That's the something special, Louise. This year we
invite all the former winners to compete for the
fiftieth anniversary of the pageant. It'll be the
Catoosa County Christmas Queen Reunion Pageant! And, of
course, my Catoosa County Catfish Farms will be the
sponsor again this year. We'll make it bigger and
better than it's ever been.
LOUISE
This is one of your more ridiculous ideas.
BUCK
You think?

LOUISE

Yes, Buck, I do. I believe this is even more ridiculous
than making the contestants do the production number
with catfish tails attached to their leotards.

BUCK

It sells catfish, Louise.

LOUISE

I don't even know why I'm going to bother making these
calls, but it's your show and Louise's Limelight
Theater isn't getting any richer so O.K., whatever you
want. But don't plan on any of them saying, yes.

BUCK

Louise, with women you just never can tell.

YOU CAN NEVER TELL ABOUT A WOMAN

YOU CAN TELL ABOUT THE WEATHER
IF IT'S GOING TO RAIN OR SHINE
YOU CAN FIGURE ON THE MARKET
AND YOU'RE APT TO GET A LINE
YOU MAY HANDICAP THE HORSES
AND PERHAPS YOU'LL DOPE THEM OUT
BUT TO FIGURE ON A WOMAN
IS TO ALWAYS BE IN DOUBT
THE TROUBLE IS YOU CAN'T TELL WHAT THEY WANT
FROM WHAT THEY SAY
AND WHAT THEY WANT TOMORROW ISN'T
WHAT THEY WANT TODAY
IF YOU DO WHAT THEY TELL YOU
WHY YOU ONLY MAKE THEM MAD
IF YOU DO THE OPPOSITE
YOU'RE SURE TO GET IN BAD
FOR YOU NEVER CAN TELL ABOUT A WOMAN
PERHAPS THAT'S WHY WE THEY'RE ALL SO NICE
YOU NEVER FIND TWO ALIKE ANY ONE TIME

AND YOU NEVER FIND ONE ALIKE TWICE
YOU'RE NEVER VERY CERTAIN THAT THEY LOVE YOU
YOU'RE OFTEN VERY CERTAIN THAT THEY DON'T
THE MEN MAY FANCY STILL
THAT THEY HAVE THE STRONGEST WILL
BUT THE WOMEN HAVE THE STRONGEST WON'T
FOR YOU NEVER CAN TELL ABOUT A WOMAN
PERHAPS THAT'S WHY WE THEY'RE ALL SO NICE
YOU NEVER FIND TWO ALIKE ANY ONE TIME
AND YOU NEVER FIND ONE ALIKE TWICE
YOU'RE NEVER VERY CERTAIN THAT THEY LOVE YOU
YOU'RE OFTEN VERY CERTAIN THAT THEY DON'T
THE MEN MAY FANCY STILL
THAT THEY HAVE THE STRONGEST WILL
BUT THE WOMEN HAVE THE STRONGEST WON'T

Scene 2

Dressing room. Skye is standing with her arms
crossed, clearly upset. Louise is sitting in a
chair near the counter, sewing on a costume.

SKYE
I am the reigning Catoosa County Christmas Queen. I am
supposed to have my final walk, sing a sappy song about
how much everybody's gonna miss me being queen and-
LOUISE
Actually, it's supposed to be a sappy song about how
much YOU'RE going to miss being the queen.
SKYE
Whatever. Then I'm supposed to crown the new queen. And
by the way, these rules need to change. I don't
understand why I can only serve one term. It's not like
it's the same as being President.
LOUISE
The President is actually allowed to serve two terms.
SKYE
I think I should be able to be queen for two terms
then. I could be queen two years just like the
President.
LOUISE
Two of his terms equals eight years.
SKYE
NOW you're talking. If the president can be president
for eight years, then I don't know why I couldn't be
the Christmas Queen for eight years.
LOUISE
Well, even if we allowed you to compete, Jolene,
there's no guarantee you'd win.
SKYE
PUH LEEZE! And stop calling me Jolene. I told you I
changed my name to Skye the day I turned eighteen.

LOUISE

That must really hurt your Momma's feelings. She's the biggest Dolly Parton fan I've ever met. Besides, Skye just sounds so Hippie-ish.

SKYE

It's not Hippie-ish! I also changed my middle name while I was at it to "Isthelimit."

LOUISE

Please tell me that's not true and that you're just being dramatic.

SKYE

(Very dramatically)

I'm not being dramatic Miss Louise!

LOUISE

Here we go.

SKYE

How in tarnation am I supposed to win more pageants or go to Atlanta and become a famous actress with the name, Jolene?

LOUISE

I guess the same way you would as Skye.

SKYE

Isthelimit, don't forget.

LOUISE

Whatever, the fact is you can be in the reunion pageant but you can't enter the regular pageant again once you've won.

SKYE

Miss Louise, I don't think you understand. I was born to be a pageant queen!

PAGEANT QUEEN

I'VE BEEN IN PAGEANTS SINCE I'S IN THE WOMB

MOM WAS PREGNANT AND WON MISS DOGWOOD
BLOOM
I HAVE A CLOSET OF SEQUINED GOWNS
AND SHALLOW THOUGHTS BENEATH MY RHINESTONE
CROWN
BUT I DON'T CARE WHAT THE PEOPLE SAY
I'VE GOT A SHERRI HILL DRESS AND HEELS THAT SLAY
I WAS BORN TO BE A PAGEANT QUEEN
MISS PIG JIG, MISS CRAWDAD, MISS COTTON PICKIN
QUEEN
I DUCT TAPE MY BOOBS AND I VASELINE MY TEETH
I KEEP MY SOCIAL MEDIA NON-OBSCENE
NO SEX OR DRUGS I AM SQUEAKY CLEAN
SWIMSUIT COMPETITION MAKES ME A WORKOUT
FIEND
I WIN CROWNS, AND TROPHIES, AND SCHOLARSHIPS
AND JUST LAST WEEK I WON MISS SHRIMP AND GRITS
OF THE CAROLINA COAST
AND VERY SOON I'LL BE MISS ALABAMA GOAL POST
SOME PAGEANTS MAKE YOU HAVE A TALENT
SOME GIRLS HAVE THEM BUT OTHERS HAVEN'T
SOME TWIRL BATONS AND DO ACROBATICS
THERE'S TAP DANCING, SINGING AND BAD
DRAMATICS
MY FRIEND GRACE DID WHAT SHE WAS ABLE
HER MOMMA WAS A WAITRESS SO SHE SET A TABLE
I WAS BORN TO BE A PAGEANT QUEEN
MISS PIG JIG, MISS CRAWDAD, MISS COTTON PICKIN
QUEEN
I DUCT TAPE MY BOOBS AND I VASELINE MY TEETH
I KEEP MY SOCIAL MEDIA NON-OBSCENE
NO SEX OR DRUGS I AM SQUEAKY CLEAN
SWIMSUIT COMPETITION MAKES ME A WORKOUT
FIEND
I WIN CROWNS, TROPHIES, AND SCHOLARSHIPS

BIG CASH PRIZES AND DON'T YOU KNOW
COLLEGE IS ALREADY PAID FOR, AND GRADUATE
SCHOOL SKYE'S THE LIMIT'S MOMMA DIDN'T RAISE NO
FOOL
AH HA HA HA AH HAA......

Scene 3

Dressing Room. Louise is sitting in a chair near
the counter. A very pregnant CeCe is standing.

CECE
You have to let me in this reunion pageant. First prize
is two thousand dollars and each contestant is getting
two hundred just to participate?! Either way I could
decorate the nursery with all that money and then some.
LOUISE
It would just be the tackiest thing in the world to let
a pregnant woman enter the Christmas Queen Pageant.
What are you thinking?
CECE
Jolene's mother was pregnant when she entered the Miss
Dogwood Bloom Pageant.
LOUISE
She was four weeks pregnant. And no one found out until
later. And we're not supposed to call her Jolene
anymore.
CECE
Why not? Lord I hope she never gets a job at a bank.
LOUISE
Why don't you want her getting a job at the bank? She'd
make a fine teller. She just needs a little more
practice counting things.
CECE
The real Jolene was a bank teller where Dolly Parton
and her husband lived. And apparently it got back to
Dolly that her husband would get in Jolene's line, EVEN
when the other tellers were free.
LOUISE
No!
CECE
Yes! So, Dolly got scared Jolene was going to TAKE HER

MAN!

LOUISE

Well our Jolene changed her name to Skye. Skye Isthelimit Newcomb.

CECE

Is that legal?

LOUISE

Apparently so. I did a little reading on it and people change their names to weird stuff all the time. One man wanted to be a politician so he changed his name to "None of the above." When he ran for office, that's how his name appeared on the ballot. He figured if folks hated all the people running, he would be a shoe in.

CECE

That's crazy!

LOUISE

Like a fox!

CECE

True. Who wouldn't want to vote for none of the above?

LOUISE

Crazy, but legal if you can believe it. You know the designer, Ralph Lauren? That isn't his real name.

CECE

It isn't?

LOUISE

Nope. He changed it. His real name was Ralph Lifshitz and he said everybody made fun of him growing up. Can you imagine wearing a designer Lifshitz outfit?

CECE

Right now, I don't think I'd give a Lifshitz. Everything I wear just looks like a big sack anyway.

LOUISE

Aww, CeCe. I think pregnant women are more beautiful than anything else in the world.

CECE

Ah huh. People just say that to us because they feel
sorry for us.

LOUISE

They're might be some truth to that. But you'll lose
that baby weight in no time after your little cherub
arrives.

CECE

Thanks Miss Louise.

LOUISE

I guess you can be in the reunion pageant. You were one
of the best Christmas Queens we ever had. Who knew that
when we couldn't find the keys to the truck for
the parade float you'd be able to hot wire it just in
time to get us in line.

CECE

I thank my Daddy every day for teaching me so many
practical things in life.

Scene 4

Dressing Room. Belva is sitting in a chair near
the counter. Louise is standing, hanging costumes
on a rack.

BELVA
A pageant? Really, Louise? At my age?
LOUISE
It's not just any ole pageant. It's a reunion pageant.
It's special.
BELVA
I don't care how special it supposedly is.
LOUISE
You were one of our first Catoosa County Christmas
Queens and it wouldn't seem right if you didn't
participate in the reunion pageant, especially
considering the fact that you still live right here in
Catoosa County. You wouldn't even have to travel
anywhere.
BELVA
Can you not see I'm as old as Methuselah?
LOUISE
Oh, come on Belva. You know nobody lives to be that old
anymore. God saw that those old codgers did nothing but
get into trouble so he sent the flood to wipe 'em out.
Now I admit you're definitely on the upper end of how
long people live today, but you're no Methuselah.
BELVA
Was that supposed to convince me?
LOUISE
I'm just saying it's a blessing to be as old as you
are. Not everyone is so lucky.
BELVA
Lucky? Most of my friends have kicked the bucket and
I'm left here to do things like represent the infirm in

a beauty pageant.

LOUISE

You are far from infirm. I know you've been going to senior goat yoga so don't tell me you're suddenly infirm.

BELVA

I couldn't resist. Those little goats are so cute. It doesn't even feel like exercise.

LOUISE

I'm just not sure I want a goat crawling all over me.

BELVA

It's fun. It's the only thing that makes all that stretching and breathing bearable. I don't even care when they pee on my yoga mat.

LOUISE

That is disgusting.

BELVA

Well, don't come crying to me when you fall and break a hip and I'm at a Disco with my Wanderlust Widows living it up.

LOUISE

Can we get back to discussing the pageant? Besides, you get two hundred dollars just for participating and if you win, it's two thousand.

BELVA

Well you didn't say there was money involved.

LOUISE

You could pay for a lot of goat yoga with that.

BELVA

True. Or it could go into my Wanderlust Widows account.

LOUISE

Wanderlust Widows? What in Heaven's name is that?

BELVA

It is a group of ladies I travel with. Mayleen Edwards organizes it. Every month we head out on an adventure.

LOUISE
What in the world does Mayleen consider an adventure?
BELVA
It can be something as simple as going to a movie or
something as big as going to Germany for Oktoberfest.
LOUISE
You're kidding.
BELVA
Nope. Wanderlust Widows is one of the best things to
happen to Catoosa County in a quite a while. We all
finally have something to look forward to instead of
sitting around wondering if our kids are gonna stick us
in a home anytime soon.
LOUISE
Do you have to be a widow? I'm sure there are old
spinsters out there that might want to join y'all. Or
even ladies who just want to get away from their
husbands for a few days.
BELVA
Wanderlust Widows doesn't discriminate against dead
husbands or live ones.
LOUISE
You know what? A night on the town to the Catoosa
County Christmas Queen Reunion Pageant could be one of
Wanderlust Widows' big monthly to do's. You could tell
Mayleen all about it and she could put it on the
schedule. I'm sure they'd be happy to come support one
of their own.
BELVA
I didn't think about that. Local getaways are getting
harder to come by. We've gone to the movies, eaten at
all the local restaurants, including the Dairy Queen,
and drunk wine made from honey at the new Meadery thing
outside of town. And by the way, wine made from honey
tastes just like beer to me. I considered it false

advertising when Mayleen said we were going wine
tasting right here in Catoosa County.

LOUISE

Mead is supposed to be the mother of beer and wine so I
guess it could really go either way. But I honestly
don't want to be drinking something cave men considered
a treat. I'm pretty sure we've come a long way since
then.

BELVA

We even went to Old Man Lumberton's dairy farm and
milked cows. Apparently milking a cow is a big thing on
folks' bucket lists.

LOUISE

Well, hell they could have come to my house at five
o'clock every morning when I was growing up and milked
old Pepper Jack. I could have slept in.

BELVA

I've got to admit, even I was a little excited. Old Man
Lumberton has taken just a few of his acres and started
some agri -tourism thing. In the fall he has hay rides,
sells pumpkins, has a haunted house, and a corn maze.
Other times of the year he has crazies like us pay him
ten dollars a piece to let us milk one of his cows. He
said he's let his soybean fields just go to hay and is
living off "dumb city people." At least that's how he
put it.

LOUISE

Little did he know Mayleen Edwards was going to get
together a group of dumb Catoosa County locals to take
out there too.

BELVA

Hey! I'm one of those dumb locals, remember?

LOUISE

I'm sorry Belva. I didn't mean that. How did we even
get off on that tangent anyway? I hate to admit it, but

I really need you to do this pageant. You know the
Limelight, like most theaters, is hurting for money and
I can't lose this pageant or its sponsorship money.

BELVA

Well, coming to shows here at The Limelight is one of
the highlights of our Wanderlust Widows outings. I'd
hate to see it go out of business.

LOUISE

Does that mean you'll do it?

BELVA

Yes. Count me in. This old queen ain't dead yet.

Scene 5

Louise is sitting at the dressing room counter
writing in a notebook. Norma Faye is thumbing
through some of the costumes on the rack. She
holds a few skimpy things in front of her.

NORMA FAYE
A reunion pageant? I've never heard of such a thing.
LOUISE
It was Buck's idea not mine.
NORMA FAYE
Since when does he go sticking his nose in the pageant
business? Shouldn't he just stick to catfish?
LOUISE
Don't be too quick to judge. That catfish sponsorship
is the reason we have the pageant every year and it
helps keep Louise's Limelight Theater afloat. If he
wants a Catoosa County Christmas Queen Reunion Pageant
then that's what he's gonna get.
NORMA FAYE
Louise, have you really thought this through? How are
people gonna react to a bunch of old queens sashaying
around on stage in a swimsuit?
LOUISE
Yes, I have thought this through. The reunion pageant
won't be having a swimsuit division. It will be
replaced with a Christmas Sportswear Division.
NORMA FAYE
What in the world do you consider "Christmas
Sportswear?"
LOUISE
Well, I've been looking into other pageants with themed
sportswear divisions that match the title of their
pageant, like the Miss Sweeter Than Candy Pageant-

NORMA FAYE

Miss Sweeter Than Candy? You know that pageant title is
a lie.

LOUISE

Anyway, the Miss Sweeter Than Candy contestants have to
wear an outfit that represents their favorite candy for
the sportswear division. I saw outfits with lollipops
or peppermints stuck to them. One girl was wrapped in
cellophane like a jolly rancher and there were Sour
Patch Kid costumes...

NORMA FAYE

All you'd have to do to look like a Sour Patch Kid is
get your momma to water you down and roll you in sand.
Those things are coated in so much sugar. But, my kind
of candy.

LOUISE

The Miss Pig Jig Contestants have to wear famous pig
appropriate sportswear.

NORMA FAYE

What is famous pig appropriate sportswear?

LOUISE

Your costume has to represent one of the world's most
famous pigs to qualify.

NORMA FAYE

How many famous pigs could there possibly be?

LOUISE

Think about it, Norma Faye. There's Porky Pig, Wilbur,
Miss Piggy, Pumba, Piglet...oh, and the pig from The
Piggly Wiggly. I'm not sure about his name.

NORMA FAYE

Who knew there were so many famous pigs?

LOUISE

The Pig Jig is one of the South's biggest festivals.
That pageant has over two hundred contestants every
year-

NORMA FAYE

All fighting for the honor of being named Miss Pig Jig.

LOUISE

That's right and laugh if you want to but not only does the winner get a five thousand dollar check, she gets a Christmas ham every Christmas for LIFE!

NORMA FAYE

That doesn't sound too bad. Now the Miss Pig Jig Pageant I'd consider, since there's money involved, not to mention all that ham.

LOUISE

Well I forgot to tell you there's money involved in the Christmas Queen Reunion Pageant.

NORMA FAYE

Now you're talking.

LOUISE

It's not as much as The Pig Jig Pageant but the winner gets two thousand dollars.

NORMA FAYE

Two thousand dollars?!

LOUISE

Yes, and two hundred just for participating.

NORMA FAYE

Hmm. What about a free Christmas ham for life?

LOUISE

I don't know if we can talk Buck into that, but he might consider a Christmas Catfish meal for life.

NORMA FAYE

That would really sweeten the deal for this old Christmas Queen.

LOUISE

I'll see what I can do.

NORMA FAYE

You never said what the "Christmas Sportswear" would be.

LOUISE

You have to be clad in something Christmasy, like an angel, snowman, reindeer, elf....something that is associated with Christmas.

NORMA FAYE

Fruitcakes are associated with Christmas. You're saying I could dress up like a fruitcake for the sportswear division?

LOUISE

That's ridiculous and frankly considering you suggested it, you wouldn't even have to dress up if you wanted to appear as a fruitcake.

NORMA FAYE

What about a can of cranberry sauce? Scrooge? A turkey? Mrs. Claus? Egg nog?

LOUISE

I don't care if you dress up as old St. Nick himself. It just won't be a swimsuit.

NORMA FAYE

Thank goodness.

LOUISE

You're welcome.

NORMA FAYE

I guess I'm in then.

LOUISE

(Let's out an enormous sigh)

Scene 6

Allie is looking at her butt in the
mirror in the dressing room.

ALLIE
Last time I was in this dressing room my butt was half
this size. Apparently, you bring a lot more home from
college than useless knowledge.

Louise enters holding a large Christmas deer lawn
ornament.

LOUISE
I'm sorry I kept you waiting Allie. The Junior League
Christmas Jingle Ball needed a few more decorations for
the VFW. I would say it takes a village but it really
just takes a few eccentric hoarders in town to attempt
to make the Catoosa County VFW look like a winter
wonderland. Between Louise's Limelight Theater's prop
room and Joe Billingsley's drive through Trailer Park
Holiday Extravaganza, we've accumulated enough
Christmas stuff through the years to make you think
Catoosa County really is the North Pole.
ALLIE
Is that Rudolph?
LOUISE
No, I think this might be Blitzen. He was caught
between a giant hairspray can and an enormous French
chandelier. I've already put the rest of the team on
the lawn to be picked up.
ALLIE
It's a good thing you have a lot of storage space.
LOUISE
Honey, if I ever retire, I'm having the world's biggest
garage sale and I'm gonna go live in one of those tiny

houses. I never want to see another prop, costume, or
set piece for the rest of my life.

ALLIE

Sounds like you've got a classic case of burnout.

LOUISE

I shouldn't be bombarding you with all my mess. I could
never burn out on theater. I think I'm just burning out
on the buck always stopping with me. For once I'd like
to do a show that I don't have to direct, sew the
costumes for, build the set for, and sell the tickets
for. I could just focus on my lines and songs and leave
the rest to someone else.

ALLIE

Miss Louise, I didn't know you were an actress.

LOUISE

I don't think anyone does. I've been behind the scenes
so long I'd almost forgotten myself. Enough talk about
me. What do you think about the reunion pageant?

ALLIE

You know Miss Louise, I shudder to think that in my
younger years-

LOUISE

You mean last year?

ALLIE

I mean, before I went off to college.

LOUISE

Uh oh.

ALLIE

I honestly can't believe I pranced around on stage in
an evening gown allowing three strangers to judge me
like I did.

LOUISE

Allison Pettigrew, those were not three strangers.
Eldon Murphy has been servicing your family's vehicles
for ages. Clementine Feltman taught you dance from the

time you were in preschool and Gertrude Farber has been the pianist in your church since you were Christened.

ALLIE

Anyway, I can't believe that I subjected myself to that and I shouldn't have thought it was O.K. to have entered such a vile exploitation of women in the first place.

LOUISE

You didn't look like you felt too exploited when you were sitting up on that decorated tractor in every parade that year. You didn't even get upset when we had to spray you down a little in the fourth of July parade because that fur trimmed cape almost made you have a heat stroke.

ALLIE

Well all I can say is, that was then, and this is now.

COOPER enters.

COOPER

Oh, I'm sorry Miss Louise. I didn't realize you were busy.

LOUISE

Come in Cooper. I told you we'd meet at three and I'm sticking to it. Allie, this is Cooper Jones, Catoosa County's newest resident. Cooper, this is Allison Pettigrew, resident FemiNazi.

ALLIE

Miss Louise!

LOUISE

I'm sorry, newly enlightened college graduate who once held the title of Catoosa County Christmas Queen.

COOPER

Oh, so you'll be one of the contestants I'll be shooting in the pageant.

ALLIE

Shooting?! What?!

COOPER

Oh! Shooting, as in with my camera. I'm an aspiring filmmaker.

LOUISE

Cooper has been hired by the Catoosa County Development Authority to shoot a promotional video and they're including highlights from the pageant.

ALLIE

A promotional video for what?

COOPER

(Flatly and rote, as if he's heard it a
thousand times but doesn't believe it)

To highlight the plethora of opportunities, benefits, and perks that Catoosa County can offer to anyone looking for an exciting- but quiet, safe, bucolic place to live.

LOUISE

Cooper here is our resident filmmaker. He's gonna be famous one day, mark my word.

COOPER

Awe, thanks. (to Allie) I'm not a filmmaker yet, but I'm hoping to be one day.

LOUISE

Don't be modest. He's got a degree from Savannah College of Art and Design and he's done some amazing work for folks around here.

ALLIE

You went to SCAD?

LOUISE

Yes he did and let me tell you, Eleanor Porter's House of Hair has increased its business twenty percent with the promotional video Cooper did for it.

COOPER
Thank you, Miss Louise.
ALLIE
I'm impressed.
COOPER
Well, don't be. My real job is starting up the tractor
paddlewheels that aerate Buck Jackson's catfish ponds.
A lot of people don't realize those catfish need oxygen
to breath.
ALLIE
Hey, an artist's got to eat.
COOPER
Unfortunately, I eat catfish for pretty much every
meal. And, you know... They're bottom feeders.
ALLIE
You may be feeding on bottom feeders today but tomorrow
you could rise to the top!
COOPER
That's a nice thought.
LOUISE
Too bad Allie's commitment to her new feminist views
will prevent her from being in our exciting pageant
that will be filmed by the world's next Scorsese.
ALLIE
I have no idea what she's talking about...(whispers)
early dementia, I'm pretty sure. I'm a contestant in
the reunion pageant so it looks like we'll be working
together. I just hope you'll remember me when.
COOPER
Wow. That makes me really happy. I'm beginning to think
pursuing film isn't just a pipe dream. Thanks for that.
ALLIE
You're more than welcome.
COOPER
You know, my dad is so wrong about women. They are good

for more than cooking and cleaning and ..... you know.

Cooper looks embarrassed and quickly exits.

LOUISE
Are you not worried about what your feminist friends
are going to think about you being in a pageant?
ALLIE
Not really. I figure it's nobody's business what I do
when it comes down to it.

AIN'T NOBODY'S BUSINESS IF I DO

IF I SHOULD TAKE A NOTION
TO JUMP INTO THE OCEAN
IT AIN'T NOBODY'S BUSINESS IF I DO
IF I DISLIKE MY LOVER
AND LEAVE HIM FOR ANOTHER
IT AIN'T NOBODY'S BUSINESS IF I DO
IF I GO TO CHURCH ON SUNDAY
AND CUSS ALL DAY ON MONDAY
IT AIN'T NOBODY'S BUSINESS IF I DO
IF I LET ME BEST COMPANION
DRIVE ME RIGHT INTO A CANYON
IT AIN'T NOBODY'S BUSINESS IF I DO
IF MY BEST FRIEND AIN'T GOT NO MONEY
AND I GET WEAK AND SAY TAKE ALL MINE HONEY
IT AIN'T NOBODY'S BUSINESS IF I DO
AND IF I GIVE HER MY LAST NICKEL
AND I KNOW IT'LL LEAVE ME IN A PICKEL
IT AIN'T NOBODY'S BUSINESS IF I DO
IT AIN'T NOBODY'S BUSINESS IF I DO
IT AIN'T NOBODY'S BUSINESS IF I DO
AND I WILL

Scene 7

Buck is standing center. There is a "Welcome to the Catoosa County Airport" sign nearby. He is holding up a sign on a stick that says "Tammy Jo." After a few moments, Tammy Jo enters with a small suitcase.

TAMMY JO
Were you afraid you wouldn't recognize me?
BUCK
Not at all. I was afraid you wouldn't recognize me.
TAMMY JO
You still look just like quarterback Buck Jackson of the Catoosa County Devils to me.
BUCK
Believe it or not, we're now the Catoosa County Fighting Catfish.
TAMMY JO
You've got to be kidding.
BUCK
It wasn't me. Reverend Jessup at The Primitive Baptist Church said the Catoosa County Devil mascot was a tribute to Satan. Nobody cared enough to fight it since neither the Catoosa County Devils or Fighting Catfish have won many games lately. Most people thought the name change may break a curse or something.
TAMMY JO
Of course that makes perfect sense to me. There aren't many folks in Hollywood that still have a healthy respect for the Devil, or curses.
BUCK
You know, I can't believe you came back home for the pageant.
TAMMY JO
Well, since my Momma and Daddy passed away, I really

haven't had a reason. It wasn't that I didn't want to.
BUCK
We're all thrilled you agreed to come.
TAMMY JO
Even Louise?
BUCK
OK, almost all of us.
TAMMY JO
I never told you how sorry I was about Anna Lee. She
was such a good soul. You two were the perfect couple.
BUCK
Thanks. She thought a lot of you. She always said
everybody was ugly with envy over your success and they
ought to be ashamed.
TAMMY JO
That's so sweet.
BUCK
I can't believe you're staying at The Only Motel in
Catoosa.
TAMMY JO
I've always thought that was the most clever name for a
motel. I always wanted to stay there.
BUCK
I stayed there once.
TAMMY JO
You're kidding.
BUCK
Nope. One summer my mother said she was tired of seeing
us swim in a catfish pond. That it was uncivilized, and
that just once she wanted us to see what it was like to
swim in a nice pool. So, she checked us into the-
TAMMY JO
The Only Motel in Catoosa.
BUCK
Marketing genius. I swam in a real pool that weekend.

TAMMY JO
And?.... Did you end up building a big swimming pool
after you built a catfish empire?
BUCK
No. If I want to cool off, I just jump in a catfish
pond. I'm sure Momma is rolling over in her grave.
TAMMY JO
Staying true to your catfish king roots.
BUCK
I'll have you know I've diversified and turned forty
acres into four hundred. I now also have cattle so I
won't hold it against you if I see you eat a hamburger
while you're here.
TAMMY JO
I'm a vegetarian.
BUCK
Not a problem. I've got a beautiful crop of soybean
coming in.
TAMMY JO
Now we're talking.

Buck holds out his hand to allow Tammy Jo to walk
off first.....like a true gentleman. They both
exit.

Scene 8

Skye, CeCe, Belva, Norma Fay, and Allie are
standing in two lines. They each have a large
catfish tail tied around their waist. Louise is
holding a clipboard. She looks at her watch and
taps her foot.

LOUISE
I should have known the prima donna was going to be
late this morning.
ALLIE
Miss Louise, it might be nine o'clock in Georgia but
it's only six o'clock California time.
NORMA FAYE
That's true Louise. Cut the woman some slack. Her
flight got in late and she's staying at The Only Motel
in Catoosa. She'll probably end up with bed bugs. Those
are probably the original mattresses they had when they
opened.
SKYE
Eww!
CECE
I gotta tell y'all. I might make this catfish tail a
permanent part of my wardrobe until the baby comes.
It's really evening out the weight in front. I swear
it's taken all the pressure off my sciatica. It's like
a Christmas miracle.
SKYE
Can we go ahead and learn the choreography and just let
this lady catch up later?

Tammy Jo enters holding her catfish tail,
disheveled. During the next lines she struggles to
tie it on.

TAMMY JO
I am so sorry I'm late. I called for an Uber-
BELVA
An Uber?
TAMMY JO
Yes. I guess I just assumed it wouldn't be an issue.
LOUISE
And you know what you get when you ASSume.
TAMMY JO
I'll tell you what I got. I got a young man riding up
to The Only Motel in Catoosa on his daddy's peanut
combine.
ALLIE
He's my brother! The whole Uber thing was my idea. I
had too much to drink one night at The Bait and Brew
and I needed a ride. He's only thirteen so he's not old
enough to drive a car but he's legal to drive a
tractor. He's been earning a lot of money so he can buy
a new deer rifle.
TAMMY JO
Thirteen, driving a giant piece of machinery, and
shooting a high-powered rifle. What could go wrong?
LOUISE
Now listen here (sultrily) "Dr. Devereaux." We don't
want to hear any of your California crazy you've
brought back with you.
TAMMY JO
I'm sorry. I guess I just thought heavy equipment,
prepubescence, and a high-powered rifle might be a bad
combination.
LOUISE
You wouldn't think it was a bad combination if the
grocery store ran out of food, now would you?

TAMMY JO
(Begrudgingly)
No. I'd be thankful. I ate plenty of game in my younger
years. God rest their little furry souls.
BELVA
Allie, you know he's not supposed to be driving that
tractor on the highway.
TAMMY JO
Oh no! We never hit the highway. We came over hill and
dale to get here. I've got the bruises to prove it. And he
got twenty-five dollars toward his new deer rifle.
NORMA FAYE
There's nothing like the smell of capitalism in the
morning.
LOUISE
That is enough of that. It is time to get this
rehearsal for the production number underway. I hope
everyone watched the choreography video I sent. I knew
we'd be on a very abbreviated rehearsal schedule so
thank heavens for the internet.
TAMMY JO
I hope I get this right. I haven't had a lot of time to
rehearse.
SKYE
I thought you were supposedly a professional?
TAMMY JO
Well, I am a professional actress, but dancing isn't
really my forte. I'm going to give it my best shot
though.
SKYE
I'm a triple threat.
NORMA FAYE
A threat to what?
SKYE
A triple threat. A person who has three essential

things in their field they excel at.
ALLIE
Oh yeah. Like a football player who's good at passing, kicking, and running.
TAMMY JO
I've never really branched out much beyond acting.
SKYE
And you call yourself a performer?
TAMMY JO
I usually just say soap opera actress. That way the expectations are pretty low.
SKYE
I can sing, dance AND act. That's why I'm a triple threat. So, step out of my way old woman.
LOUISE
Time for your whiskers, ladies. (Louise hands out the catfish whiskers.)
CECE
What in the world?
LOUISE
Just put it on honey. It'll really help cover up all that hair on your top lip.
CECE
What???!! (She rubs her upper lip.)
BELVA
Don't worry. It's just one of the joys of pregnancy. Most of it will go away after the baby comes.
CECE
Most of it?!
LOUISE
5,6,7,8

During the number Skye moves Tammy Jo out of the way so that she can be in front.

SUWANEE, HOW I LOVE YA

I'VE BEEN AWAY FROM YOU A LONG TIME
I NEVER THOUGHT I'D MISSED YOU SO
SOME HOW I FEEL
YOU LOVE IS REAL
NEAR YOU I LONG TO WANNA BE
THE BIRDS ARE SINGIN', IT IS SONG TIME
THE BANJOS STRUMMIN' SOFT AND LOW
I KNOW THAT YOU
YEARN FOR ME TOO
SWANEE! YOU'RE CALLING ME!
SWANEE!
HOW I LOVE YOU, HOW I LOVE!
MY DEAR OL' SWANEE
I'D GIVE THE WORLD TO BE
AMONG THE FOLKS IN
D-I-X-I-E-VEN NOW MY MAMMY'S
WAITING FOR ME
PRAYING FOR ME
DOWN BY THE SWANEE
THE FOLKS UP NORTH WILL SEE ME NO MORE
WHEN I GO TO THE SWANEE SHORE!
THE BIRDS ARE SINGIN', IT IS SONG TIME
THE BANJOS STRUMMIN' SOFT AND LOW
I KNOW THAT YOU
YEARN FOR ME TOO
SWANEE! YOU'RE CALLING ME!
SWANEE, SWANEE, I AM COMING BACK TO SWANEE!
MAMMY, MAMMY, MERRY CHRISTMAS!

Scene 9

Tammy Jo and Buck are eating dinner and having margaritas at "Tequila Mockingbird." There is a banner that says, "Christmas Karaoke Tonight."

TAMMY JO
It's nice to see Tequila Mockingbird still in business and going strong.
BUCK
Yeah. We might still have only one motel in town but we've acquired quite a few new restaurants. Of course none can hold a candle to Tequila Mockingbird.
TAMMY JO
Remember in the tenth grade this place was our Spanish class field trip?
BUCK
Yes. I guess a trip to our local Mexican restaurant was as close as a lot of kids were ever going to get to going to another country. I got to ask our waiter his name, order "dos" tacos and ask him where the library was.
TAMMY JO
All I remember is Joe Wheeler asked in Spanish where the bathroom was and then was so impressed with himself he kept yelling, Yo soy impotente! Yo soy impotente!
TAMMY JO
Which of course he thought meant, I am awesome. Then Senora O'Connor yelled, Sit down Joe! It's one thing to be awesome but entirely another to be impotent.
BUCK
Impotente, imponente. I can see the confusion.
TAMMY JO
And clearly poor Joe did not.
BUCK
How did rehearsal for the production number go today?

TAMMY JO
You don't want to know.
BUCK
That bad, huh?
TAMMY JO
I don't think Skye's the Limit likes me very much.
BUCK
Ah yes, Jolene. I don't think Jolene likes anybody but
Jolene very much, so you really shouldn't be very
offended.
TAMMY JO
It's just that when people hate me right off the bat
and don't even know me, it's upsetting.
BUCK
You think maybe they confuse you with your character?
TAMMY JO
Most definitely. When my character had an affair with
that young orderly, no matter where I went, all I could
hear was people making cougar sounds when I walked by.
One lady even stopped me at McDonald's and said I was a
cradle robber and they shouldn't let me anywhere near
the play place!
BUCK
But you know you're not Veronica Devereaux, (makes
cougar noise.) Sorry, I couldn't resist.
TAMMY JO
Yeah, but it's not always that. I doubt Skye is a big
fan of Hot Springs General Hospital.
BUCK
I think it's sweet.
TAMMY JO
You think what's sweet?
BUCK
That you actually care what some small-town girl thinks
about you.

TAMMY JO
I guess I kind of care what everybody thinks about me
if it's not true.
BUCK
Well, I know the real you and frankly you seem to still
be the same down to earth girl you were in high school.
Hollywood hasn't changed you.
TAMMY JO
It's funny that a lot of people have this grand vision
of what my life is like, when the reality is, I'm on
set for twelve hours most days with a lot of boring
down time. So, I'm pretty good at Sudoku and Solitaire.
I then get take out or microwave a lean cuisine and
curl up on the couch with my cat.
BUCK
Oh my God, that is so pathetic.
TAMMY JO
What?!
BUCK
I'm kidding! But you're doing what you love and isn't
that what life's all about?
TAMMY JO
I used to love it when I was younger but as I've gotten
older, I really just want to cook some new recipes and
ride horses. Boring, right?
BUCK
It doesn't really matter what I think. It just matters
what you think will make you happy. I know what will
make me happy.
TAMMY JO
You do? And what is that?
BUCK
If you kick off Christmas Karaoke tonight at Tequila
Mockingbird. Besides, none of the people in here have

taken their eyes off you since we walked in the door. (Buck looks at the audience.)

TAMMY JO
Absolutely not. I haven't sung since high school chorus.
BUCK
I remember. It was my favorite class. No homework. Come on. Get us all in the Christmas Spirit.
TAMMY JO
I am not going to sing Christmas Karaoke at Tequila Mockingbird. Besides, I've only had one margarita.
BUCK
Waiter! Could I get a pitcher of margaritas....Thank you! Show the world that you've got more in you than being a doctor with a fetish for young interns. (Buck starts a chant.) Tammy Jo! Tammy Jo! Tammy Jo! (He gets up and looks at the audience and indicates for them to join.) Tammy Jo! Tammy Jo! Tammy Jo!
TAMMY JO
You will pay for this.

Tammy Jo approaches the "stage" area decorated with a Christmas Karaoke banner. She takes a hand held microphone.

WHAT CHILD IS THIS? (MARTINA MCBRIDE STYLE)

WHAT CHILD IS THIS, WHO, LAID TO REST
ON MARY'S LAP, IS SLEEPING?
WHOM ANGELS GREET WITH ANTHEMS SWEET
WHILE SHEPHERDS WATCH ARE KEEPING?
THIS, THIS IS CHRIST THE KING
WHOM SHEPHERDS GUARD AND ANGELS SING
HASTE, HASTE TO BRING HIM PRAISE
THE BABE, THE SON OF MARY

SO BRING HIM INCENSE, GOLD, AND MYRRH
COME PEASANT KING TO OWN HIM
THE KING OF KINGS, SALVATION BRINGS
LET LOVING HEARTS ENTHRONE HIM
THIS, THIS IS CHRIST THE KING
WHOM SHEPHERDS GUARD AND ANGELS SING
HASTE, HASTE TO BRING HIM PRAISE
THE BABE, THE SON OF MARY
OH, RAISE, OH RAISE A SONG ON HIGH,
HIS MOTHER SINGS HER LULLABY.
JOY, OH JOY FOR CHRIST IS BORN,
THE BABE, THE SON OF MARY.
THIS, THIS IS CHRIST THE KING
WHOM SHEPHERDS GUARD AND ANGELS SING
HASTE, HASTE TO BRING HIM PRAISE
THE BABE, THE SON OF MARY
THE BABE, THE SON OF MARY

Scene 10

Belva, Louise, and Skye are in the dressing room.
Belva is putting on her wrist leis. She is dressed
in anything from a leotard with tights to a
Christmas sweater and pants. She has on a grass
skirt, head leis, a leis necklace, and she is
barefoot. Preferably the leis will be red and
green. Skye has on her costume for her tap dance
and her tap shoes. She is stretching and Louise is
sewing on a costume. Allie leans in the door to
the dressing room.

ALLIE
Miss Belva are you about ready? CeCe is almost
finished.
BELVA
Yes, hon. Did you say Cooper is filming this rehearsal?
ALLIE
Yes. That's in case somebody decides their rehearsal
performance is better than the real thing. They can
choose and he'll just edit out the bad one and edit in
the good one.
BELVA
You young whippersnappers and your amazing technology.
Too bad we can't go back in life and edit out bad
marriages and bad perms.
ALLIE
See you out there.
Belva walks out the dressing room door and emerges
back on the stage standing toward the audience.
BELVA
Retirement has been good to me. I just got back
from a vacation with my group Wanderlust Widows.
We went to Hawaii and attended a traditional Luau.

I was amazed at those hula dancers and how they
shook what the Good Lord gave them. Now when I
first entered The Catoosa County Christmas Queen
Pageant, way back when, I danced the mashed
potato. My days of dancing the mashed potato are
over although we are still intimately connected.
These days everything I eat has the consistency of
mashed potatoes. I've decided to dance again as my
talent. This time I'm gonna do a Hawaiian
Christmas Hula. I hope I make my Wanderlust Widows
proud.

WHEN SANTA COMES TO HA-WA-II

WHEN SANTA COMES TO HA-WA-II
ALL THE LITTLE DOLPHINS GO SQUEAK SQUEAK
SQUEAK
HE DOESN'T COME RIDING ON A SLEIGH
BUT BY KAY AH LA KAY KOO AH BAY
AND SAILING ON AN OUTRIGGER CANOE
OR A SURFBOARD YELLING COWABUNGA DUDE!
WHEN SANTA COMES TO HA-WA-II
ALL THE DOLPHINS GO SQUEAK SQUEAK SQUEAK
Dance Interlude
WHEN SANTA COMES TO HA-WA-II
ALL THE LITTLE DOLPHINS GO SQUEAK SQUEAK
SQUEAK
AND HE DOESN'T COME RIDING ON A SLEIGH
BUT BY KAY AH LA KAY KOO AH BAY
AND SAILING ON AN OUTRIGGER CANOE
OR A SURFBOARD YELLING COWABUNGA DUDE!
WHEN SANTA COMES TO HA-WA-II
ALL THE DOLPHINS GO SQUEAK SQUEAK SQUEAK
EVERYTHING IS SO OH OH SWEET
WHEN SANTA...COMES TO HA-WA-II!

Scene 11

Skye and Louise are in the dressing room. The last eighteen seconds of Stars and Stripes Forever plays. When it ends....

TAMMY JO (O.S.)
Dang it!

Tammy Jo enters the dressing room. She is wearing a red, white, and blue obnoxious costume holding a baton.

LOUISE
What was that all about?
TAMMY JO
I dropped my two turn! I never drop the two turn. It almost feels like somebody put some oil or something on my baton.
SKYE
Maybe you're a little rusty...after ALL THESE YEARS.
LOUISE
Personally, I don't know why you care so much. It's just rehearsal. You'll do fine during the actual pageant then you'll be off back to California, land of the crazies.
TAMMY JO
I don't really care about winning or not, but I don't want to make a complete fool of myself.
SKYE
Well, that's already been achieved with just your outfit. It really doesn't matter if you ever touch the baton.
LOUISE
Cool it Jolene. I won't have any bickering among my contestants. Besides, don't forget you're all vying for

that Miss Congeniality award. The winner gets a one hundred-dollar gift certificate to Friendly's Bar and Grill.

SKYE

I don't really need that but Tammy Jo slash Dr. Veronica Devereaux might.

TAMMY JO

And why exactly would you say that?

SKYE

Well, as far as anyone knows you've never been married and you don't have a boyfriend, so unless you'd prefer a gift certificate to Lickety Split's Lesbian Bar in Birmingham, you're really the one who needs that gift certificate to Friendly's so you can pick up a man.

TAMMY JO

If I really wanted a man, I'd have a man.

SKYE

Hmm. If you're such a big star why haven't you ever been married?

TAMMY JO

Because I choose not to be.

SKYE

YOU choose? Or no one has chosen to ask you?

TAMMY JO

I choose.

SKYE

Ah huh.

TAMMY JO

I like being free and single. This way the world is my oyster.

LOUISE

Ah huh.

TAMMY JO

I have complete freedom. I can just run wild. I'm completely free to do whatever I want whenever I want to.

LOUISE

Methinks she doth protest too much. That's Hamlet in case you don't recognize it.

TAMMY JO

Think whatever you want.

RUNNIN' WILD

RUNNIN' WILD, LOST CONTROL
RUNNIN' WILD, MIGHTY BOLD
FEELIN' GAY, RECKLESS TOO
CARE FREE MIND ALL THE TIME, NEVER BLUE
ALWAYS GOIN' DON'T KNOW WHERE
ALWAYS SHOWIN', I DON'T CARE
DON'T LOVE NOBODY, BUT ME WORTH WHILE
ALL ALONE, AND RUNNIN' WILD.
NO MAN IS GONNA MAKE A FOOL OF ME
NO MAN! I MEAN JUST WHAT I SAY
I'M NOT THE SIMPLETON I USED TO BE
WONDER HOW I GOT THAT WAY
ONCE I WAS FULL OF SENTIMENT, IT'S TRUE
BUT NOW I'VE GOT A CRUEL HEART
WITH ALL THAT OTHER FOOLISHNESS I'M THROUGH
GONNA PLAY A WOMAN'S PART
I'M RUNNIN' WILD, LOST CONTROL
RUNNIN' WILD, MIGHTY BOLD
FEELIN' GAY, RECKLESS TOO
CARE FREE MIND ALL THE TIME, NEVER BLUE
ALWAYS GOIN' DON'T KNOW WHERE
ALWAYS SHOWIN', I DON'T CARE
DON'T LOVE NOBODY, BUT ME WORTH WHILE
ALL ALONE, AND RUNNIN' WILD

LOUISE
All that's fine and dandy but my friend Carlos at
Tequila Mockingbird overheard you tell Buck that
you just go home to your cat every night.
Louise and Skye laugh. Tammy Jo looks livid.

Scene 12

Tequila Mockingbird. Tammy Jo and Buck are seated
at a table. Allie and Cooper are at a table. Norma
Fay, Belva, and CeCe are seated together.

ALLIE
You're doing a great job creating the promotional video
for Catoosa County.
COOPER
Thanks. I've got good material to work with. You ladies
in the reunion pageant give me a lot of good fodder.
ALLIE
I think that was supposed to be a compliment.
COOPER
O.K., fodder may have not been the best choice of
words. You guys give me a lot of great material to work
with.
ALLIE
That's definitely better.
COOPER
It wouldn't be half as good if you weren't acting as
host on the video.
ALLIE
Well, I certainly never thought I'd use my broadcast
journalism degree in Catoosa County while I was waiting
to get a job in a big city.
COOPER
I hope you don't mind but I sent out some cuts of our
Catoosa County promo video to some businesses and they
asked if I could do some work for them but they said
only if you did the interviews and stuff.
ALLIE
You're kidding.
COOPER
You've got a real talent. I'd say better even than Ryan

Seacrest, Oprah Wynfrey or Kelly Rippa, and she's super hot.

ALLIE

I guess we make a pretty good team.

COOPER

I don't think there's any guessing to it. I propose we be business partners.

ALLIE

Business partners it is!

COOPER

What should we call ourselves?

ALLIE

Hmm. Allie and Cooper..... Hmm. I've got it. Alley-Oop productions!

COOPER

Sounds like a slam dunk to me!

BUCK

Was rehearsal any better today?

TAMMY JO

Maybe a little. The ladies are really sweet with the exception of Jolene of course.

BUCK

She was always a devil child.

TAMMY JO

She apparently hasn't changed much.

BELVA

Ladies, it's time to get our karaoke on!

NORMA FAYE

Oh No! Y'all know I don't sing. I even mouth the hymns in church.

BELVA

Fine. CeCe, get your tail up on that stage and let's spread some Christmas cheer.

CECE

Looks like it's the only cheer I'm getting for a while.

Y'all know how bad a virgin margarita tastes?
NORMA FAYE
A heavily pregnant woman forced to drink virgin drinks.
Oh, the irony.

Belva and CeCe stand under the Christmas Karaoke
banner and begin to sing. As they sing everyone
casually takes to the dance floor joining in a
group "electric slide" type dance.

JOLLY OLD ST. NICHOLAS

OO OO OO OO....
JOLLY OLD SAINT NICHOLAS, LEAN YOUR EAR THIS
WAY,
DON'T YOU TELL A SINGLE SOUL WHAT I'M GOING TO
SAY.
CHRISTMAS EVE IS COMING SOON,
NOW YOU DEAR OLD MAN,
WHISPER WHAT YOU'LL BRING TO ME, TELL ME IF YOU
CAN.
OO OO OO OO
JOLLY OLD SAINT NICHOLAS, LEAN YOUR EAR THIS
WAY,
DON'T YOU TELL A SINGLE SOUL WHAT I'M GOING TO
SAY.
CHRISTMAS EVE IS COMING SOON,
NOW YOU DEAR OLD MAN,
WHISPER WHAT YOU'LL BRING TO ME, TELL ME IF YOU
CAN
TELL ME, TELL ME, TELL ME IF YOU CAN
TELL ME, TELL ME, TELL ME IF YOU CAN
TELL ME, TELL ME, TELL ME IF YOU CAN
TELL ME, TELL ME, TELL ME IF YOU CAN

Scene 13

Louise and Skye are in the dressing room. Skye has
on a leotard and catfish tail and is stretching.
Louise is hanging costumes on a rack.

SKYE
I can't believe the pageant is tomorrow.
LOUISE
I'll be glad when it's over and the umpteenth
presentation of A Christmas Carol can commence.
SKYE
How are people not sick of that play?
LOUISE
I have no idea, but it sells like hotcakes.
SKYE
We get it. Scrooge was bad. There are three ghosts and
a crippled boy. Been there done that.
LOUISE
All I know is there's usually no drama backstage unlike
the Christmas Queen Pageant.
SKYE
I guess that's true. Remember last year when Kaitlin
and Hannah got into it. Kaitlin secretly changed Hannah's
talent song to Hard Hearted Hannah the Vamp of Savannah
and told everyone that Hannah was a call girl.
LOUISE
Well, Kaitlin was just trying to get her revenge after
Hannah rubbed that chocolate bar on the butt of
Kaitlin's bikini before the swimsuit competition.
SKYE
Everybody was convinced Kaitlin had a bad nervous
stomach.
LOUISE
Then Melba Jenkins who's always had a weak stomach
vomited right on the judge's table.

SKYE

It was the right thing to disqualify them.

LOUISE

Of course it was and it helped your chances of becoming Christmas Queen.

SKYE

EXCUSE ME?

LOUISE

Had it not been for that chocolate racing stripe on Kaitlin's swimsuit, she'd have probably won swimsuit and had enough points to beat you out.

SKYE

I think not eating carbs is a mental disorder so she should have probably been disqualified anyway.

LOUISE

Whatever.

Belva, CeCe, Norma Fay, Allie, and Tammy Jo enter the dressing room. The ladies all casually greet one another. They all take off their coats and begin putting on their catfish tails. Tammy Jo begins to look under things etc. for her tail.

TAMMY JO

Has anyone seen my tail? It was hanging on the rack when I left last night.

SKYE

Honestly, I don't know why you're so worried about it.

TAMMY JO

What do you mean?

SKYE

You're going to lose anyway. And when I beat out the famous Dr. Veronica Devereaux for Christmas Queen, everyone in Hollywood is going to wonder what I have that you don't.... You know, besides a lot of years ahead of me.

Skye flits off. Belva approaches her.

BELVA
Not so fast young lady. I've seen many folks struck
down in the prime of their life and you need to know
that you're not immune.
SKYE
What are you talking about?
BELVA
I'm just saying I'd sleep with one eye open if I were
you.
NORMA FAYE
Belva!

Belva returns and has a seat at the counter.

NORMA FAYE
Belva, you need to be careful, we're too old to get
into a cat fight.
BELVA
Honey, I know I'm not a contender anymore that's why I
keep my friends Smith and Wesson close by.
NORMA FAYE
Belva!
BELVA
I know my cat fightin' limits these days. That's all!

Tammy Jo is still frantically searching for her
catfish tail.

TAMMY JO
I'm telling y'all. I hung it up before I left last
night.

LOUISE
Well, maybe you should take better care of your props.
TAMMY JO
I carefully hung the tail!
LOUISE
Alright. Don't get your panties in a wad. I'll see what
I can find.

Louise exits the dressing room.

TAMMY JO
And for the record, my panties are not in a wad!
BELVA
Nobody can describe being mad better than a southerner.
TAMMY JO
I'm not mad. I'm just frustrated.
ALLIE
As frustrated as a snake that married a garden hose.
NORMA FAYE
It's fine Tammy Jo. Everybody throws a little hissy fit
every now and then.
TAMMY JO
I'm not throwing a hissy fit!!!

All the ladies stare at her because of her
outburst.

CECE
Now don't pee down my back and tell me it's raining.
TAMMY JO
What?!

Louise enters carrying a devil tail.

LOUISE
This is all I could put my hands on. It was left over
from the Halloween show.

Skye comes over to gloat. Louise is holding the
devil tail and standing between Skye and Tammy Jo.

.
TAMMY JO
(to Skye)
You'd better hope I don't find out you had something to
do with this.
SKYE
What are you gonna do if I did? I will snatch you bald
headed, lady.
TAMMY JO
Oh yeah? And I will cancel your birth certificate.
SKYE
I will knock you into the middle of next week.
TAMMY JO
Well, you'd better give your heart to Jesus because
your butt is mine!

A catfight between Tammy Jo and Skye ensues as the
lights go down.

INTERMISSION

ACT 2

Scene 1

Norma Faye is out front in a pair of cowboy boots and western attire. Belva, Skye, CeCe, Allie, and Tammy Jo are standing behind her singing while Norma Faye finishes a western line dance to Up on the Housetop a la Reba McEntire. Belva, Skye, CeCe, Allie, and Tammy Jo already have on their Christmas Sportswear Division attire.

UP ON THE HOUSE TOP (END)

LOOK IN THE STOCKING OF LITTLE BILL
OH, JUST SEE WHAT A GLORIOUS FILL
HERE'S A HAMMER AND LOTS OF TACKS
WHISTLING BALL AND A WHIP THAT CRACKS
HO, HO, HO! WHO WOULDN'T GO? HO, HO, HO! WHO
WOULDN'T GO?
UP ON THE HOUSETOP, CLICK, CLICK, CLICK
DOWN THROUGH THE CHIMNEY WITH GOOD SAINT
NICK

Everyone applauds, hoops, and hollers. Norma Faye bows. Everyone Exits. Louise enters with a hand held Mike. (After each contestant finishes her walk she stands on opposite sides of the stage so that all contestants are left on stage at the end of the Christmas Sportswear Division.)

LOUISE
(sarcastically)
My, my... that was just.... somethin' else. Thank you Norma Faye for that display of... talent. (rolls her eyes.) Next, ladies and gentlemen. We have something

very special. Instead of the Swimsuit in December
Division of the Catoosa County Christmas Pageant, we
will have a Christmas Sportswear Division. I mean,
after all, this is the Reunion Pageant and the last
thing folks would want to see is one of our older
queens traipsin' around in a swimsuit.

BELVA (O.S.)
I heard that!

LOUISE
Anyway, without further ado, the Catoosa County
Christmas Queen Reunion Pageant Christmas Sportswear
Division!

As Louise introduces each lady, she does the
famous T Pageant walk. Of course, Skye embellishes
each stop with a turn. Other ladies add their
personality. Ex. CeCe might not be well balanced
in her shoes since she's pregnant. Norma Faye
probably wears her cowboy boots with her Christmas
outfit, etc. Louise reads from her note cards on
each contestant.

LOUISE
First up is contestant number one, CeCe Whitlow. CeCe
enjoys spending time with her husband, Billy Ray and
her pit bull Cujo - Oh Lord, hide the baby - Her
favorite foods are saurkraut, buttermilk and cornbread,
and oysters. I'm assuming this is a temporary favorite
foods list. Thank you, CeCe. Next, we have our oldest
Catoosa County Christmas Queen.

BELVA
Was that really necessary?

LOUISE
Miss Belva Pike. Belva enjoys traveling the world or
just Catoosa County with her cohorts in The Wanderlust

Widows. Belva enjoys (Louise stares at the card.) sword swallowing, nude sunbathing, and deciphering ancient Egyptian hieroglyphics in her spare time. Good Lord. Belva wishes for world peace but in all her years she realizes there are too many "bleep"holes in the world for that. Belva Pike, ladies and gentlemen. Moving ON!

SKYE

My turn America!

LOUISE

Our reigning Miss Catoosa County Christmas Queen is here for this special Reunion Pageant. Miss Skye Isthelimit Newcomb. Some of you will remember her by her God given name "Jolene."

SKYE

Louise! Stick to the script!

LOUISE

Skye enjoys volunteering her time rehabilitating wild baby birds that have been covered with oil from oil spill environmental catastrophes - Jolene, Catoosa County is landlocked and five hours from the coast!

SKYE

(through a clenched smile)

Just read the script Louise!

LOUISE

She has given her hair to Locks of Love three times already this year - Nobody's hair grows that fast! Jolene charges over to Louise and snatches the microphone.

SKYE

I'd like to give a shout out to the children I tutor at Catoosa County Alternative School for Crazy Kids. I've put in 9,000 volunteer hours this year and enjoyed every second.

LOUISE

Give me that microphone. There aren't 9,000 hours in a

year! NEXT we have Allison Pettigrew. Allie has just partnered with Cooper Tatum to create Allie-Oop Productions providing Catoosa County and beyond with quality promotional videos. Allie would like to further explain to those who've asked, that she and Cooper do not create pornographic videos and never will, UNLESS one day they choose to consummate their love and do so in the privacy of their own home, for their own enjoyment?! What?!

ALLIE
Well, I didn't want to lie about it. My mother always said, "You should never say never because eventually you'll probably just end up a liar."

LOUISE
I'm too old for this. Norma Faye Jones is up next. Norma Faye was our only Catoosa County Christmas Queen to place in the State Christmas Queen pageant.

Norma Faye stands at the start of the "T" and doesn't move.

SKYE
I'd just like everybody to know, the state pageant went out of business so I couldn't compete. Because Sky Isthelimit Newcomb would have certainly been a shoe in to win.

LOUISE
Yes, the state pageant got busted for smuggling drugs inside breast implants, so they got shut down by the DEA. I mean, Merry Christmas, right?

NORMA FAYE
Can I go now?

LOUISE
Yes, we can't get this over fast enough. Norma Faye is the sole proprietor of Norma Faye's Lair of Love on the

outskirts of Catoosa County. Come spice up your love life with gifts from Norma Faye's Lair of Love with a ten percent Christmas Discount. -Do you not have a hobby or something I can talk about?

Norma Faye gives Louise a look.

LOUISE
Oh, for Heaven's sake! Norma Faye would like everyone to know that she is opening an additional Lair of Love location in Willacoochee, just two counties over. Our next and final contestant and no we did not save the best for last. The ladies drew their numbers out of a hat. Anyway, our final contestant is Miss Tammy Jo Fordham who has traveled all the way from California to participate in the Catoosa County Christmas Queen Reunion Pageant. Why, I have no idea.

Tammy Jo begins her T.

LOUISE
Tammy Jo moved to California to pursue a career in acting, if that's what you want to call it, starring in Hot Springs General Hospital for most of her career. (coughs)Soap opera slut.
TAMMY JO
I heard that!

Tammy Jo is only halfway finished with her T walk. Louise shoves her over into the line with the others.

LOUISE
And those are our contestants in the Sportswear Division of the Catoosa County Christmas Queen Reunion

Pageant.

Scene 2

Louise enters with the hand-held microphone.
Allison doesn't bother changing out of her
Christmas Sportswear Costume although one vital
piece may be removed.

LOUISE
Next, we will be wowed by the talent of Miss Allison
Pettigrew, who is (reads the card silently, confused.
She yells toward "backstage.") I thought you were
playing the trombone?
ALLIE (O.S.)
My lips are sore.
LOUISE
Cooper! Come out here!

Cooper enters with lipstick smeared all over his
mouth.

Get back behind that camera or I will tell the Chamber
of Commerce.
COOPER
I'm sorry Miss Louise. That was very unprofessional.

Cooper exits.

LOUISE
And I'm telling your Momma! Moving right along. Allison
Pettigrew will be presenting, "How to Cook the Perfect
Turkey." Take it away, Allison.

Allie enters with an aluminum roasting pan,
baster, measuring cup, meat thermometer, alarm
clock, aluminum foil, carton of broth etc. and the
bird itself, if you have one, and a CELL PHONE.

ALLIE

Since this is a Christmas pageant and most folks
cook a Turkey on Christmas Day, I decided that for
my talent I would demonstrate to all you good
folks, how to cook the perfect turkey. This year
happened to be the first time I hosted my family
at my house for Thanksgiving. Around my age, women
have to take their first turn at cooking a giant
bird that they've never cooked before in their
lives, however, that first cooked turkey will be
on display for all your family and friends, so the
pressure is on. For years I've listened, to first,
my grandmother talking about waking up every two
hours the night before Thanksgiving to "BASTE THE
BIRD!" I realize now why she looked like the wild
woman of Borneo every Thanksgiving Day, while my
Great Aunt Pearl, who never married and cooked for
a family of her own, showed up every year looking
like an AARP model. After my grandmother retired
from turkey duty, the job fell to my mother. I got
to hear her moan from the kitchen about how dry
and how absolutely not fit to eat the turkey was.
So ladies, today I will stand before you, a girl
from a long line of turkey basting southern
belles, and demonstrate how to cook the perfect
turkey. As you can see I have all the ingredients
along with the obligatory alarm clock, which would
help me get up every hour on the hour, to ensure
the bird is good and moist. BUT, I won't be
needing any of this for our feathery friend.
Because this Catoosa County Christmas Queen will
now show you the secret to the perfect turkey.
(She pulls out her cell phone.) Hello?... Piggly
Wiggly? I'd like to pre order a fully cooked
turkey with all the fixins... (She puts her hand

over the receiver of the phone and loudly whispers
to the audience..) Or, you could just have
catfish. (Flashes a Great Big Pageant Smile.)
LOUISE
Thank you, Allie for that display of.... forsaking
everything your southern Momma taught you. Next, we have
Jolene performing-
SKYE (O.S.)
Skye!
LOUISE
Skye Isthelimit Newcomb performing a vocal and tap
dancing talent to I Love a Piano. This pageant is going
to be the death of me..

Louise exits looking defeated. Skye enters in an
outlandish costume complete with wrist gauntlets
and headpiece.

SKYE
I LOVE A PIANO

AS A CHILD I WENT WILD WHEN A BAND PLAYED
HOW I RAN TO THE MAN WHEN HIS HAND SWAYED
CLARINETS WERE MY PETS,
AND A SLIDE TROMBONE I THOUGHT WAS SIMPLY
DIVINE
BUT TODAY WHEN THEY PLAY I COULD HISS THEM
EV'RY BAR IS A JAR TO MY SYSTEM
BUT THERE'S ONE MUSICAL INSTRUMENT THAT I CALL
MINE
I LOVE A PIANO, I LOVE A PIANO
I LOVE TO HEAR SOMEBODY PLAY
UPON A PIANO, A GRAND PIANO
IT SIMPLY CARRIES ME AWAY
I KNOW A FINE WAY TO TREAT A STEINWAY

I LOVE TO RUN MY FINGERS O'ER THE KEYS, THE
IVORIES
AND WITH THE PEDAL I LOVE TO MEDDLE
NOT ONLY MUSIC FROM BROADWAY
I'M SO DELIGHTED IF I'M INVITED
TO HEAR A LONG-HAIRED GENIUS PLAY
SO YOU CAN KEEP YOUR FIDDLE AND YOUR BOW
GIVE ME A P-I-A-N-O, OH, OH
I LOVE TO STOP RIGHT BESIDE AN UPRIGHT
OR A HIGH TONED BABY GRAND
I LOVE A PIANO, I LOVE A PIANO
I LOVE TO HEAR SOMEBODY PLAY
UPON A PIANO, A GRAND PIANO
IT SIMPLY CARRIES ME AWAY
I KNOW A FINE WAY TO TREAT A STEINWAY
I LOVE TO RUN MY FINGERS O'ER THE KEYS, THE
IVORIES
AND WITH THE PEDAL I LOVE TO MEDDLE
NOT ONLY MUSIC FROM BROADWAY
I'M SO DELIGHTED IF I'M INVITED
TO HEAR A LONG-HAIRED GENIUS PLAY
SO YOU CAN KEEP YOUR FIDDLE AND YOUR BOW
GIVE ME A P-I-A-N-O, OH, OH
I LOVE TO STOP RIGHT BESIDE AN UPRIGHT
OR A HIGH TONED BABY GRAND

LOUISE
Ladies and Gentlemen, we have arrived at our glorified
bathroom break which everyone in theater refers to as
intermission. We have activities going on in our lobby
courtesy of Buck Jackson's Catoosa County Catfish Farms
Incorporated. There's Bobbing for Baby Catfish, and new
this year is a sniff contest to see who can correctly
identify all flavors of Catfish Charlie Blood Bait,
Wildcat Cheese Dip, Type B Blood Flavor, Full Stringer,

and Pole Cracker. Please know this contest is not for the faint of heart, or those with prior heart conditions. See you back here in fifteen minutes.

Scene 3

Tammy Jo is in the dressing room. She has on her evening gown. Buck knocks.

BUCK
You decent?
TAMMY JO
Come on in.
BUCK
I just wanted to say thank you for agreeing to come back and be in this pageant. I know some of the ladies have been pretty tough on you.
TAMMY JO
Hollywood gave me calluses like you can't imagine.
BUCK
I bet. It's tough out there, huh?
TAMMY JO
These ladies are like pussy cats compared to some casting directors and my fellow actresses.
BUCK
I've heard it's a dog eat dog world out there.
TAMMY JO
Dog eat dog, lion, mouse and everything in between.
BUCK
Why do you stay?
TAMMY JO
I'm beginning to ask myself the same thing.
BUCK
I guess you really love coming home to that cat.
TAMMY JO
Very funny. You know, it's nice being in a theater and not on a set. I did some stage acting to pay the bills before I landed the role of Dr. Devereaux and I really miss it.

BUCK

Who knows? Maybe Louise will cast you in one of the shows next season as a special guest and you could come back for another visit.

TAMMY JO

I'd like that.

BUCK

I could sweeten the deal by being a sponsor, maybe.

TAMMY JO

That would be hard to say no to. Instead of Hot Springs General Hospital which is usually sponsored by diaper, and laundry detergent manufacturers, I could tell folks I've graduated to Catfish Farm sponsors.

BUCK

Clearly a step up. Well, break a leg during your talent.

TAMMY JO

You're even learning the lingo!

BUCK

Believe it or not, I know about a little more than catfish. Anna Lee used to drag me to the Fox to see every musical under the sun. We even went to New York a few times to see some Broadway shows.

TAMMY JO

And?

BUCK

(a pause)

I have to admit, I didn't hate it.

TAMMY JO

Not exactly a resounding endorsement.

BUCK

O.K. I actually really enjoyed it. I'm a fan.

TAMMY JO

No wonder you're such a big supporter of Louise's Limelight Theater.

BUCK
Secret's out. Again, break a leg.
TAMMY JO
I'll try.

Scene 4

Louise enters.

LOUISE
Our next division is evening gown slash interview and
our first contest is Ms. Belva Pike.

Belva enters in a beautiful evening gown and goes
down center to Louise.

LOUISE
In honor of this being a Catoosa County Christmas Queen
Reunion Pageant our interview question is What is your
favorite Christmas memory. We figured since you've
experienced so many Christmases we would start with you
Belva.
BELVA
What?!
LOUISE
What is your favorite Christmas memory, Belva?
BELVA
I believe my favorite Christmas memory was when I was
about seven years old and Santa brought me a U NEED TO
PEE WEE DOLL. I was fascinated that I had a baby doll
that actually peed. It came with some little diapers
too...
LOUISE
And that's your favorite Christmas memory, with so many
to choose from?
BELVA
Come to think of it, that doll kinda started getting on
my nerves cause I had to change it all the time. You
know, that's probably why I didn't have my first baby
until I was thirty-five.

LOUISE
Belva Pike, ladies and gentlemen, and her favorite
Christmas memory. Thank you, Belva.

Belva exits. Norma Faye enters.

LOUISE
Next, we have Norma Faye Jones. Norma Faye please share
a memorable Christmas experience from your past with
all these fine folks.
NORMA FAYE
I would definitely have to say my favorite Christmas
memory is the first year Norma Faye's Lair of Love right
off highway 92- was open. I know that it made a
lot of couples happy that Christmas. Christmas toys
galore. It's probably the best Christmas THEY ever had
for sure.
LOUISE
NEXT!

Norma Faye exits. Allie enters.

LOUISE
Here comes Allison Pettigrew to share with us one of
her favorite Christmas memories. Allie, what would you
consider your best Christmas memory.
ALLIE
Honestly Miss Louise, I believe my best Christmas is
yet to come.
LOUISE
Aww.
ALLIE
I've just graduated from college, things are really
heating up with my and Cooper's relationship and our
new business has just taken off, so I'm thinking this

Christmas is going to be a hum dinger for sure.
LOUISE
Well that is so-

Cooper runs onto the stage.

LOUISE
Excuse me?!
COOPER
The camera is rolling Allie.
LOUISE
What is going on here?
COOPER
Could you step out of the frame, Miss Louise.
LOUISE
Good God Almighty. You have got to be kidding me.

Louise steps to the side of the stage. Cooper gets
down on one knee.

ALLIE
Oh my gosh! Is this really happening?!
COOPER
Yes, it is.
ALLIE
Wait, the other side is my better side.

Allie and Cooper switch sides. He gets back down
on one knee.

ALLIE
Do I have any lipstick on my teeth?

She opens her mouth and Cooper examines her teeth.

COOPER
Nah, you're good.

Allie fixes her hair and adjusts the bodice of her
gown.

ALLIE
I'm ready.
COOPER
I know you're a strong woman, and I respect that. And
you don't really need a man but..

He takes out a ring box. Allie snatches it out of
his hand, takes out the ring and flings the box.
Louise has to dodge the box.

ALLIE
Yes! Yes! Yes!

Cooper and Allie hug and make out as they exit.

LOUISE
Our first proposal here at the Limelight Theater folks.
And let's hope it will be our last. Up next we have
CeCe Whitlow.

CeCe enters.

LOUISE
CeCe, please, for the love of all that is good in this
world, share with us your favorite normal Christmas
memory.
CECE
My very favorite Christmas memory was the Christmas my
Daddy was deployed but came home for Christmas to

surprise us. He hid in a giant box that Momma wrapped. We couldn't believe it Christmas morning when we saw such a big present under the tree. Momma told us it was for all of us so we all started ripping the paper off and out popped Daddy. It was definitely the best Christmas of my life.

LOUISE

Well praise the Lord and pass the ammunition! Finally, a wonderful Christmas memory! Thank you, CeCe Whitlow. Now get off the stage before you ruin it.

CeCe exits.

LOUISE

Our next contestant is Jolene Skye Isthelimit Newcomb.

Skye enters.

LOUISE

Miss Newcomb, would you please describe to the judges what you consider your best Christmas memory.

SKYE

My favorite Christmas memory is when I launched my Charity – "Christmas for Cows" - since I'm a vegetarian. We deliver Christmas goodies to cows all over Catoosa County. It's not enough that it's the one time of year they don't have to live in fear because everybody's eating turkey for Christmas. "Christmas for Cows" brings Christmas cheer to our bovine friends by giving them Pilates Balls to play with, and Cabbage and Cauliflower Leaves, because at "Christmas for Cows," cows are people too.

LOUISE

Fascinating. NEXT!

Skye exits. Tammy Jo enters.

LOUISE
Our final contestant is Tammy Jo Fordham. Tammy Jo,
what would you consider your favorite Christmas memory.
TAMMY JO
Honestly, Louise, this Christmas is definitely shaping
up to be one of my favorites for several reasons,
mainly-
LOUISE
And there you have it, folks. The interview portion of
the Catoosa County Christmas Queen Reunion Pageant.

Louise shoos Tammy Jo off the stage. Tammy Jo
exits.

LOUISE
I'd like to take this time to thank this year's judges.
Mack Mabry from Mack's Auto Repair. They're slogan,
"We'll Cheat Ya Right!" Wylene Fannin from Curl Up and
Dye Hair Salon. Nobody does hair bigger and better than
Wylene. And Elaine Peabody from Let's Get Fiscal Tax
Preparers. Kicking Assets and Taking Names! Thank you,
judges!

CeCe enters. She still has on her evening gown.

LOUISE
CeCe Whitlow will now perform her talent for us. And
I'm going to have a drink.
CECE
The year I won Catoosa County Christmas Queen, I
performed an advanced gymnastics floor routine. In my
present state if I make it to the floor, my husband has
to pull me back up or I'm going to be there until this

baby comes. Since this anniversary pageant happens to be sponsored by Catoosa County Catfish Farms, I'd thought of demonstrating catfish noodling. That's when you hunt for a catfish under the edges of the river bank. You stick your arm down there, block 'em in in their hiding place and then scoop 'em up by the mouth. I figured since it was cold y'all wouldn't appreciate having to follow me outside and down the edge of the stream outback so - I'm going to stick with the Christmas Theme, keep it simple, and sing a Christmas carol.

THE WEXFORD CAROL

GOOD PEOPLE ALL, THIS CHRISTMAS TIME
CONSIDER WELL AND BEAR IN MIND
WHAT OUR GOOD GOD FOR US HAS DONE
IN SENDING HIS BELOVED SON
WITH MARY HOLY WE SHOULD PRAY
TO GOD WITH LOVE THIS CHRISTMAS DAY
IN BETHLEHEM UPON THAT MORN'
THERE WAS A BLESSED MESSIAH BORN
NEAR BETHLEHEM DID SHEPHERDS KEEP
THEIR FLOCKS OF LAMBS AND FEEDING SHEEP
TO WHOM GOD'S ANGELS DID APPEAR
WHICH PUT THE SHEPHERDS IN GREAT FEAR
"ARISE AND GO", THE ANGELS SAID
"TO BETHLEHEM, BE NOT AFRAID
FOR THERE YOU'LL FIND THIS HAPPY MORN'
A PRINCELY BABE, SWEET JESUS BORN"
WITH THANKFUL HEART AND JOYFUL MIND
THE SHEPHERDS WENT THAT BABE TO FIND
AND AS GOD'S ANGEL HAD FORETOLD
THEY DID OUR SAVIOR CHRIST BEHOLD
WITHIN A MANGER HE WAS LAID

AND BY HIS SIDE THE VIRGIN MAID
AS LONG FORETOLD UPON THAT MORN'
THERE WAS A BLESSED MESSIAH BORN

Scene 5

The dressing room. Tammy Jo is in her red, white,
and blue talent costume and is looking all around
for her baton. Skye who is wearing her evening
gown, is fixing her make up with one eye on Tammy
Jo.

TAMMY JO
My baton was right here a few minutes ago. Have you
seen it?
SKYE
I sure haven't. You don't seem to be able to keep up
with anything; your catfish tail, your baton, a man.
TAMMY JO
You know some women don't measure their worth by having
a man or not.
SKYE
But you'd think you could have snagged at least one.
TAMMY JO
I've snagged plenty. I'm just a firm believer in "catch
and release."
Louise enters.
LOUISE
What are you doing? It's time for your talent, Tammy
Jo!
TAMMY JO
I know. I'm sorry. I can't find my dad gum baton.
SKYE
Looks to me like if you can't perform your talent, then
you're disqualified.
TAMMY JO
I bet you'd love that....JOLENE!
LOUISE
I warned you two! After that crazy cat fight, y'all do
one more thing and I'm tossing both of you out of this

pageant.

TAMMY JO

No problem, Louise. One thing I learned from growing up in Catoosa County is that there is more than one way to skin a cat - OR a catfish!

Tammy Jo yanks down the curtain rod, snatches off the end finial and pulls the curtain off the rod. She wraps the curtain around her a la Scarlett and sashays out the door.

Scene 6

Tammy Jo is on the stage while Louise stands off
with her mike and cue cards.

TAMMY JO
Chance Ashby will surely arrest me since he found out
about the clone I created to bring down Erica. Thank
goodness he now has amnesia and probably won't remember
it at all. He certainly can't find out our marriage was
a sham. But since I'm about to perform brain surgery on
him, I will insert a memory chip in his brain so that
he only remembers what I want him to remember. Not our
sexcapade in the sixth floor janitor room, not my-
Someone throws a pair of boxer shorts on to the
stage. Louise storms out and picks them up.
LOUISE
Who did this? (She points to different audience
members.) Was it you? What about you? You look guilty
as sin. I'm betting it was you. Due to heathenistic
acts we're going to have to cut this contestant's
talent short, IF that's what y'all want to call it.
TAMMY JO
What?
LOUISE
I need all the contestants to please take the stage.

Belva, CeCe, Norma Faye, Skye, (not Allie) all
enter wearing their evening gowns. Tammy Jo stands
among them wrapped in the curtain.

LOUISE
Judges.
Buck enters with an envelope and a crown.
LOUISE
The sponsor of our pageant, Buck Jackson, owner of

Catoosa County Catfish Farms will do the honors.

Buck opens the envelope.

BUCK
The first runner up of the Catoosa County Christmas
Queen Reunion pageant is.... Jolene Skye Isthelimit
Newcomb!
SKYE
First runner up, my ass!

Cooper and Allie enter. Allie is trying to fix
mussed hair and straightens her dress. Cooper is
holding a catfish tail and a baton.

COOPER
Miss Louise, you know that stuff everybody was looking
for? I found it in your office while I was
ah....charging my batteries.
LOUISE
(to Cooper) What are you doing?!
TAMMY JO
It wasn't Skye that was trying to sabotage me?
SKYE
I don't need to sabotage anybody to win.
NORMA FAYE
Well, apparently you do, miss first runner up.
SKYE
UUghhh!!!!
TAMMY JO
It was you, Louise.
LOUISE
It was! I'm sorry. THREE TIMES! I entered the Catoosa
County Christmas Queen Pageant. Three times, and I
never got above first runner up. And I stayed here and

you just gallivanted off. I was jealous. You chased your dream and I stayed here.

TAMMY JO

But Louise, you've brought a lot of joy to people bringing shows here to The Limelight Theater.

LOUISE

There have been some good times.

BUCK

It's true. You've really brought culture to Catoosa County with the Limelight.

TAMMY JO

I believe no one embodies this pageant more than Louise Ledbetter. She's been hosting it for years, even giving up a prime weekend at Christmas in order to have this town's pageant. If anyone deserves to be this year's Catoosa County Christmas Queen, I believe it's her.

CECE

I agree. Miss Louise, I grew up coming to see shows like Annie, Grease, and My Fair Lady here at The Limelight. And I loved every minute of it.

NORMA FAYE

The Limelight makes for a great date night.

ALLIE

I fell in love here at The Limelight.

BELVA

Willacoochee Widows have a lot of outings here at The Limelight.

Everyone looks at Skye.

SKYE

How many times do you really need to be a Catfish Christmas Queen? Congratulations, Miss Louise.

BUCK

I believe this belongs to you.

Buck crowns Louise.

LOUISE
Do I get the prize money too?
BUCK
Absolutely!
LOUISE
Attention everyone! The Limelight Theater, as of this
moment, is for sale. I'm going to New York!
BUCK
Well, Tammy Jo, what do you think?
TAMMY JO
About what?
BUCK
You could enjoy small town living and run your own
theater. Our Main Street right here in Catoosa County
could be the South's new Broadway. What do you say?
TAMMY JO
A resounding yes!

They hug, kiss etc. Cooper brings out Louise's
suitcase.

COMPANY

IN OLD NEW YORK! IN OLD NEW YORK!
THE PEACH CROP'S ALWAYS FINE!
THEY'RE SWEET AND FAIR AND ON THE SQUARE!
THE MAIDS OF MANHATTAN FOR MINE!
YOU CANNOT SEE IN GAY PAREE,
IN LONDON OR IN CORK!
THE QUEENS YOU'LL MEET ON ANY STREET
IN OLD NEW YORK

THE END

Made in the USA
Columbia, SC
23 June 2019